Samuel French Acting Edition

Sundown, Yellow Moon

by Rachel Bonds

Music & Lyrics by The Bengsons

Additional Lyrics by Rachel Bonds

SAMUELFRENCH.COM   SAMUELFRENCH.CO.UK

FOR PRODUCTION ENQUIRIES

UNITED STATES AND CANADA
Info@SamuelFrench.com
1-866-598-8449

UNITED KINGDOM AND EUROPE
Plays@SamuelFrench.co.uk
020-7255-4302

Each title is subject to availability from Samuel French, depending upon country of performance. Please be aware that *SUNDOWN, YELLOW MOON* may not be licensed by Samuel French in your territory. Professional and amateur producers should contact the nearest Samuel French office or licensing partner to verify availability.

MUSIC USE NOTE

IMPORTANT BILLING AND CREDIT REQUIREMENTS

If you have obtained performance rights to this title, please refer to your licensing agreement for important billing and credit requirements.

SUNDOWN, YELLOW MOON was commissioned by The Writer's Room (Manhattan Theatre Club, Ars Nova). It was additionally developed by Ars Nova (Jason Eagan, Founding Artistic Director; Renee Blinkwolt, Managing Director). The world premiere was presented by Ars Nova (Jason Eagan, Founding Artistic Director; Renee Blinkwolt, Managing Director) and WP Theater (Lisa McNulty, Producing Artistic Director; Michael Sag, Managing Director).

The premiere took place in March 2017 and was directed by Anne Kauffman, with set design by Lauren Helpern, costume design by Jessica Pabst, lighting design by Isabella Byrd and Matt Frey, and sound design by Leah Gelpe. The stage manager was Erin Gioia Albrecht. The cast was as follows:

RAY (RAYLEEN) .... Lilli Cooper
JOEY (JOSEPHINE) .... Eboni Booth
TOM .... Peter Friedman
CARVER .... JD Taylor
TED DRISCOLL ....Greg Keller
JEAN .... Anne L. Nathan
BOBBY .... Michael Pemberton

CHARACTERS

RAY (RAYLEEN) – Joey's twin sister, mid-twenties.

JOEY (JOSEPHINE) – Ray's twin sister, mid-twenties.

TOM – Their dad, mid/late fifties.

CARVER – Tom's counselor, early/mid-thirties.

TED DRISCOLL – A poet, forties.

JEAN – A family friend, early fifties.

BOBBY – A family friend, mid/late fifties. This actor should also provide the voice for the **LATE NIGHT DJ**.

SETTING

In the south. In a small college town.
Somewhere very green and very humid, like Tennessee.

TIME

Late July. The thick of summer.

AUTHOR'S NOTES

A slash (/) indicates where the next character's line begins to overlap. Sometimes it happens at the beginning of a line, like: " / Hey there." Which means the two characters begin talking at the same time.

Music. All music exists within the reality of the world of the play, except for "Carver's Song," which somehow breaks the world open.

"We're all mad here."

– The Cheshire Cat

"Every man should have a daughter."

– My dad

PROLOGUE

(In the darkness, the sounds of radio static, and then the voice of the DJ *streams in, amidst the static and song.)*

LATE NIGHT DJ. – And that was a sneak peak at a haunting little gem from the Moonlight Miles – a group that got their start not far from these parts, if you can believe it... And something tells me this new record is sure to become the album of the summer... Something to get you through the long, hot days and all those dark, humid nights. Now this next one is...

PART I

1.

(**RAY** *and* **JOEY** *at the reservoir. They stare out.* **RAY** *hums.)*

JOEY. Ray you're doing the thing.

RAY. What?

JOEY. When you're humming and you don't know you're humming.

RAY. Oh – sorry.

JOEY. God, does the reservoir look so much smaller than you remember it?

RAY. Uhhhh, I don't know. Maybe.

JOEY. It looks so small to me.

RAY. Yeah.

Eughh.

JOEY. He's okay. He's not dying.

RAY. He sounded so – sad on the phone.

JOEY. He's okay.

RAY. What do you think actually happened?

JOEY. What he said. He lost his temper and said some stuff he shouldn't have.

RAY. ...Yeah, / but...

JOEY. And the school's new headmaster is some right-wing asshole and he freaked out.

RAY. Yeah, but...it must have been really bad. Dad's said some crazy shit before and nothing / happened –

JOEY. *Yeah* but this guy is new and clearly he's super uptight.

RAY. *Or* it was really, really bad.

JOEY. Like what are you imagining?

RAY. I don't know, he... – You saw how he was to Mom at Thanksgiving, / that was –

JOEY. Oh god, but that was – That's different!

RAY. That fight in the kitchen?! Just over the stupid – the potatoes or whatever – That got serious, / Joey.

JOEY. I know.

RAY. So, I'm just – saying. It could have been bad.

> (**JOEY** *nods and looks down. The girls are quiet for a brief moment.*)

JOEY. I think Dad just made some smartass comments to this headmaster guy, like went off on one of his political rants or something, and then the guy had to suspend him to prove a point.

RAY. I just hate thinking of him like – sitting at that house, alone, just, in his bathrobe...

JOEY. I know.

RAY. And that house depresses the shit out of me.

JOEY. ...Yeah, well...

RAY. There's not even a real bedroom for us.

JOEY. Why should he spend money on bedrooms when we're only there like twice / a year?

RAY. I don't know! I just thought he would.

JOEY. He needs to save money, Ray.

RAY. I know I know I know I know.
    You didn't say anything to Mom, did you?

JOEY. No.

RAY. Good.

JOEY. I mean, she knows we're visiting –

RAY. Yeah, I know / that –

JOEY. And of course she asked how he's doing.

RAY. What'd you say?

JOEY. I said he was fine. And that we're not willing to be some weird go-between for them, so...

RAY. Good.

Well.

(She stares out and exhales.)

At least we can swim while we're here.

JOEY. I need to do some work while we're here.

RAY. Oh god, come on!

JOEY. I do.

RAY. Why?

JOEY. Because it's important to me that I am prepared for the fall.

RAY. You're going to be way over-prepared.

JOEY. Ray, everyone there is fiercely intelligent, like – intimidatingly smart, so I have to do more to be / ready.

RAY. You always think that, though, and then you're the number one smartest person in the / room –

JOEY. That is not true.

RAY. AND you're a million times more prepared than anyone else.

*(**JOEY** raises her eyebrows.)*

No, but seriously, can you try to calm down a little while you're here?

JOEY. What does that mean?

RAY. Just – ease up on some of the militant behavior maybe?

*(**JOEY** looks away.)*

JOEY. What time is it?

RAY. Euughh I know we should go, we should go, he's probably wondering where we are.

*(**RAY** takes out her phone, scrolling through over and over. **JOEY** looks over at the time.)*

JOEY. Shit, yeah, we should go.

RAY. I know.

Euuuuuugh!

(She yells at her phone in frustration.)

JOEY. Whaaaat is happening?!

RAY. Nothing.

JOEY. What was that about?

RAY. Nothing, just...

JOEY. Maria?

RAY. *(Lying back, covering her face.)* No. Yes.

JOEY. What's going on with that?

RAY. Well I guess nothing, because she's – whatever, yeah
– nothing.

JOEY. *(Laughing.)* Well you should do something about
that.

RAY. I have – I mean I did!

JOEY. What'd you do? Send her an email being like, "Oh hi,
it's me, Ray, I like you, do you like me? – Check yes or
/ no –"

RAY. You're an asshole.

Anyway we should go.

JOEY. Yes. We should.

(They look at each other.)

RAY. Yeah. Okay.

Let's go.

***

2.

(Late night: **RAY** *and* **TOM**, *trying to sleep in the living room. She lies on a futon; he sleeps on the floor in a sleeping bag. Headlights flash across the wall.* **RAY** *sits up.)*

RAY. ...Dad?

TOM. Hm?

RAY. Someone's outside.

TOM. Hm?

RAY. Someone's outside.

TOM. *(Sitting up.)* What? Where?

RAY. Someone's out in front of the house, / like –

TOM. Oh – that's Carver.

RAY. Your counselor guy?

TOM. Yeah, he – Sometimes he drives by and checks in on me.

RAY. The school told him to do that?

TOM. No, no...he just does it.

RAY. That's weird.

TOM. Oh, it's not that *weird*.

RAY. It's kind of late to just be driving around, isn't it?

TOM. What can I say, the guy likes to drive around in the middle of the night.

RAY. Why?

TOM. I don't know, Ray, I imagine he gets some sort of peace from it – Helps him clear his head. His mother's sick.

RAY. What's wrong with her?

TOM. She's a shut-in. And has some dementia now too / I believe.

RAY. She doesn't leave the house at all?

TOM. Don't you love sleeping? I thought you LOVED sleeping.

RAY. What, does he like, come by and peer in your windows or something?

TOM. NO, he just drives by.

RAY. Every night?

TOM. No, not EVERY night, but, I don't know, sometimes I'm asleep.

RAY. That's weird, Dad.

TOM. Oh for Chrissakes – If he wants to drive by the house in the middle of the night, then he can drive by the house in the middle of the night. It's not hurting anyone.

RAY. Okay okay okay okay. So do you guys… What do you talk to him about?

TOM. What?

RAY. Like are you doing a program, or – How do you prove that you're "fit for public life" or whatever?

TOM. Oh Jesus, I don't know.

RAY. But is it like an anger management program?

TOM. We just talk. About little things. Books. Music. And then at the end of the twelve weeks he signs a thing that says I'm a good, completely sane guy and I go back to teaching.

RAY. Do you think he will?

TOM. Why wouldn't he?

RAY. I don't know, I'm just –

TOM. Of course he will. Because I am a good guy. And the boy likes me.

RAY. …So he comes over here?

TOM. Yes.

RAY. Why?

TOM. Because it's more private and I don't want everyone in town and at the school in my business. All right? So – let's all go to sleep.

RAY. I can't.

TOM. Try, Rayleen. Try.

RAY. This mattress is digging into my shoulder.

TOM. Oh GOD I raised some whiny kids.

RAY. I'm not whining, / I'm just –

TOM. Oh no? It sounded an awful lot like whining to me –

RAY. NO, I'm just – telling you. Tomorrow night I get your room.

TOM. We will all take turns. Goodnight, darling child, and I'm sorry about your shoulder.

RAY. Okay goodnight.

TOM. Goodnight. For the last time.

RAY. Well don't say THAT, that sounds like you're going to die in your sleep.

TOM. Jesus fucking Christ, Ray!

RAY. You were the one who said goodnight all morbidly.

TOM. It was not meant that way, believe me.

RAY. Okay, well don't say things like that, like "the last time."

TOM. What is wrong with you, girl?

RAY. I'm just – restless. Eugh – never mind, okay, goodnight.

TOM. GOODNIGHT. Sweet dreams.

RAY. You too.

> (*A long, long moment of quiet.* **RAY** *props herself up on her elbows and stares at her dad; his eyes are closed.*)

...Dad?

TOM. ...Hm?

RAY. Will you sing me something?

Sing me something?

> (*She stares at him for a long moment. His breathing is even.*)

...I'm worried.

I'm worried about you.

> (*But he's asleep.* **RAY** *flops on her back, staring at the ceiling, then tosses and turns and then lies sprawled out, again, defeated. She hums quietly to herself.*)

***

3.

(Late the next morning. **CARVER** *stands at the door.* **RAY** *is in her pajamas, standing in the doorway;* **JOEY** *ties on her running shoes very, very tightly somewhere in the background.)*

CARVER. Hey there.

RAY. Hey.

CARVER. Carver.

RAY. Yeah, right – Ray.

CARVER. Hey Ray.

RAY. Hi.

CARVER. Good to see you. Just here to meet with your dad.

RAY. He went to the grocery store.

CARVER. Oh, he did?

RAY. Yeahhh...but I'm sure he'll be back soon, / if you...

CARVER. Did he really?! That's great.

RAY. Um – yeah. But, do you want to come in, or?

CARVER. Well I don't want to bug y'all, but if you don't mind me waiting for him –

RAY. Ohhhh my god, wait – Patrick Carver.

CARVER. That's right.

RAY. Dad said "Carver" but I didn't make the – You went to St. Nick's with us.

CARVER. Uhhh, I did, yeah. But way before y'all were there, right?

RAY. No no, you were a senior when we were in middle school.

CARVER. Oh yeah? – Okay, that's right.

RAY. Yeahhh, I remember you.

CARVER. ...Yeah?

JOEY. Hi.

CARVER. Hey there.

JOEY. Joey.

CARVER. Joey, right. Carver. How're you?

JOEY. I'm good. Can I help you with something?

CARVER. I was just telling Ray here – If y'all don't mind, I was just going to wait for your dad, / till he –

JOEY. Yeah, he's at the store.

CARVER. Yes – I think I'm a few minutes early, / so.

JOEY. Though I think he said he was going to run some other errands too? Might be awhile.

CARVER. Oh – Okay, that's – Yeah, he maybe forgot we were supposed to meet.

JOEY. He didn't say anything about it.

CARVER. Huh. Well...I don't mind waiting.

RAY. Sure.

JOEY. Okay, so sorry, I'm just gonna sneak past you –

CARVER. Going for a run?

JOEY. That's the plan.

CARVER. It's real hot out already, so – be careful.

JOEY. Yeah – I got my nerdy water belt here, so I'm all set.

(She squeezes past him.)

Sorry – I'm just going to, uh –

CARVER. *(Moving out of the way.)* Oh, sure, yeah. Have fun.

RAY. Don't go for a million hours!

JOEY. *(Fading away.)* Yup!

(They watch her go.)

CARVER. Woo – She's dedicated, huh?

RAY. Yeah, she's insane.

CARVER. Y'all don't run together?

RAY. No, that's her thing.

CARVER. Ohh, okay, / gotcha.

RAY. We don't do all the same things.

CARVER. No, of course not.

RAY. Even though we're twins, we're actually very different people.

CARVER. Of course, I get that.

RAY. Sorry, I know, I'm just – Old resentment bullshit, you know.

CARVER. ...Sure.

RAY. She likes to run. I really don't.

CARVER. Hey, I'm with you. So then what's your thing?

RAY. Uhhhh.

CARVER. I thought your dad was telling me you're a musician?

RAY. Yeah, I'm – Yeah.

CARVER. You write your own songs?

RAY. Uhhhhhhhh. Kind of.

CARVER. *(Laughing.)* No?

RAY. No I do, just – truly sucking at doing it lately.

CARVER. Aw, no, I doubt that.

RAY. Eh, it's true.

But didn't you use to play?

CARVER. Uhh – a long time ago.

RAY. With the Moonlight Miles.

CARVER. Yup.

RAY. Do you talk to them still?

CARVER. Nah. I kind of...drifted. From them. And they're all famous now, / so –

RAY. I know, it's crazy.

CARVER. ...Yeah.

(He looks away, toward the door.)

You know what? Maybe I should just call your dad later on to reschedule.

RAY. Okay, I can tell him.

CARVER. Thanks Ray.

RAY. Hey, um – So is he doing okay?

CARVER. Uhhh I can't say.

RAY. Well that doesn't sound good.

CARVER. No – I'm sorry, I just don't want to be – talking about things I shouldn't, so –

RAY. Okay...

CARVER. Privacy and all, so.

RAY. Right. He's just being all shady, so I'm just trying to –
I don't know – figure out what's / going on.

CARVER. Yeah, I really can't say. I'm sorry.

> *(He looks toward the door.)*

I'm uh... So if you don't mind telling him I'll call him
to reschedule.

RAY. Oh – Sure.

CARVER. I 'preciate it, Ray.

> *(He waves and disappears. She stares after
> him.)*

***

4.

(TOM sits in the kitchen, the grocery bags on the table. RAY calls from off.)

RAY. *(Offstage.)* Dad?!

(A pause.)

TOM. ...Yeah.

(RAY comes into the kitchen. She unpacks a twelve-pack of Sprite, a dozen eggs, and a box of microwave popcorn.)

RAY. This is all you got?

TOM. Complainers. I raised a bunch of whiny complainers.

RAY. This is just a strange assortment of things...

TOM. Yeah, well I forgot to bring a list.

RAY. You know Joey doesn't eat eggs?

TOM. What the hell? That's new.

RAY. She's doing this vegan thing right now.

TOM. Good fucking god, why is she doing that?

RAY. Because she's crazy.

TOM. Well... Will she eat popcorn?

RAY. *(Inspecting the box.)* Not if there's..."movie theater butter" on it.

TOM. Well, she can eat popsicles then. I got a bunch of popsicles in the freezer.

RAY. Won't eat those 'cause of the sugar.

TOM. Oh Christ Jesus.

RAY. But can I have one?

TOM. Of course you can – yes. Grab me one too while you're in there.

RAY. What color?

TOM. Oh...orange.

(They unwrap and eat popsicles.)

RAY. Oh my god I love popsicles.

TOM. I know.

RAY. Aren't they so good?

TOM. Mm-hmm.

(**RAY** *squints at* **TOM.**)

Yes, dear?

RAY. Have you been cooking at all?

TOM. Why?

RAY. Or just eating popcorn for every meal?

TOM. I'm eating fine.

RAY. Okay.

TOM. What?

RAY. *(Shrugging.)* Nothing.

(*Stretching.*)

Eugh, I'm still tired.

TOM. Maybe because you were chattering away into all the wee hours.

RAY. Or maybe because I was sleeping on that ancient futon.

TOM. Oh god, here we go.

RAY. That thing is so old, Dad.

TOM. I know it is.

RAY. And kinda ratty.

TOM. Yes, I know, that's why I was allowed to keep it.

(**RAY** *looks at the floor.*)

RAY. You could get some new furniture.

TOM. It'll do for now.

Where'd Joey get to?

RAY. Running.

TOM. Running, huh?

RAY. Yup.

TOM. She been doing that a lot?

RAY. Not that much.

TOM. ...You'd tell me if something was going on, right?

RAY. She's fine.

TOM. Because you know I count on you to be my eyes and ears on that girl.

RAY. She's okay, Dad.

>(**TOM** *squints at her, worried.*)

Carver came by looking for you.

TOM. He did?

RAY. Did you have an appointment?

TOM. Well I thought we'd talked about rescheduling, but... Did you tell him I was at the store?

RAY. Yes, he seemed very impressed by that?

TOM. *(Rolling his eyes.)* Oh Lord.

RAY. He said he'll call you to reschedule.

TOM. Okay, that's fine.

RAY. You didn't tell me it was *Patrick* Carver.

TOM. Yes. Though he just goes by Carver now.

RAY. I know him, Dad.

TOM. Oh yeah?

RAY. He was the one that had the thing with Father Caldwell.

TOM. He was. Yes.

Please don't bring that up to him.

RAY. DAD – GOD – I would never.

But...did anyone ever find out what actually... happened?

TOM. I mean they dismissed the bastard and he was chased out of town, but who knows.

RAY. Eugh god. That's awful.

TOM. I know.

RAY. And he just still lives here? Eugh god.

TOM. Well Christ Ray.

RAY. No, I just mean – with everyone knowing that about him.

TOM. Please don't be a snob like your mother, that's all I ask of you.

RAY. Dad, Jesus. She's not a snob.

TOM. Oh no? She sure liked to look down her nose at folks around here.

RAY. Yeah, well it wasn't easy for her living here.

TOM. I know that.

RAY. Do you?

TOM. I do, Ray.

RAY. Okay... Well, I just *meant*. That he seems sad, that's all.

TOM. I know.

RAY. *(Shaking it off.)* Anyway, ummmm – Do you want to go swimming today? Joey and I are gonna go out to the reservoir.

TOM. Oh, yeah, y'all should go. They built a new dock down there.

RAY. But we want you to come.

TOM. Aw, that's – Nah, I'll just stick around here.

RAY. No, but that's the whole point. To go together...

TOM. I know, darlin', I'm just – not in the swimming mood I guess. I should do some work anyway.

RAY. What work?

TOM. I have to prepare for the fall.

RAY. But you don't know if they're even bringing you back.

TOM. Baby, I will be teaching in the fall.

RAY. But you don't know that yet, do you?

TOM. Ray, darling child, what do you know about it?

RAY. Well not enough, because you won't tell us what actually happened!

TOM. I've told you! And it's completely ridiculous, the whole / thing, so –

RAY. So then why did they suspend you?

TOM. Because the new headmaster is a narrow-minded right-wing whackjob and we disagree on almost all counts on how to educate, / so –

RAY. So what happened?

TOM. Well, your dad just –. Lost his temper, as he does sometimes. And he did something he shouldn't have.

RAY. Like he...?

TOM. Like he screamed obscenities real loud at the headmaster in front of a whole bunch of kids.

RAY. That's it?

TOM. ...Well, as he continued to yell and gesticulate wildly at the very patronizing things the whackjob was saying, the very nice World History teacher, who also happens to be the man's wife, came over to try to remedy the situation –

RAY. Oh god.

TOM. And your father *very* mistakenly backhanded her with a great deal of force.

RAY. *(Covering her face, quiet.)* Oh god. Dad.

TOM. Gave her a real shiner too.

...So it was all really very embarrassing and horrible, as you can see. And now I'm drowning in the consequences, / so...

RAY. *(Quiet.)* Yeah.

(A pause.)

TOM. Please PLEASE please do not tell your mother.

RAY. I won't.

TOM. I can't... I cannot have her knowing.

RAY. I mean, I think she would get it if you explained / it to h–

TOM. DO NOT tell her, Ray, I'm asking you.

RAY. Okay.

(He shakes his head, looking down.)

TOM. ...So – Enough. Why don't y'all go swimming and we'll make dinner together after? I'll see if Bobby and Jean want to come round to play. I'm getting pretty good on that guitar, now – You'll see.

RAY. Oh yeah?

TOM. Yes ma'am, Bobby's been teaching me some things.

RAY. That's great.

TOM. You brought yours with you, right?

RAY. I left it in the city.

TOM. Well why in the hell'd you do that?

RAY. *(Shrugging.)* Don't know.

TOM. I'm sure you can borrow one of Bobby's. I'll ask.

RAY. ...Okay.

TOM. Sound like a plan?

RAY. Yeah. But we're gonna need to go back to the grocery store.

TOM. *(Hanging his head.)* Oh shit, you're right. Euughhhhh Christ.

RAY. But Joey and I can go after we swim.

TOM. Oh, thank you. I fear I don't have another trip in me today.

> *(He touches her shoulder, then shuffles toward his bedroom.)*

RAY. Where are you going?

TOM. Gonna go back to sleep for a bit.

RAY. It's past noon.

TOM. I know, but I didn't sleep too well either last night. Wake me up when y'all come back from swimming.

RAY. ...Okay.

TOM. Thanks, gal.

> *(He nods and shrinks into his room. She opens the fridge, staring at its emptiness. A little flower of worry blooms in her gut. She sharply closes the fridge and stands alone in the kitchen, the worry blooming larger.)*

***

5.

(**RAY** *and* **JOEY** *make their way through the woods to the reservoir.*)

RAY. Dad hit a woman in the face.

JOEY. What?!

RAY. That's what happened. He got in a fight with the headmaster and was yelling and I guess waving his arms around and accidentally backhanded the headmaster's wife right in the face.

JOEY. (*Laughing.*) Holy shit!

RAY. It's not funny Joey – He hurt her.

JOEY. No no, I know, it's just – I mean it's kind of funny.

RAY. He gave her a black eye.

JOEY. God.

RAY. It's bad, Joey.

JOEY. Ohh, but it was obviously an accident, they can't make / that –

RAY. He gave her a black eye.

JOEY. But not on purpose, Ray, obviously.

RAY. I don't know.

JOEY. Ray.

RAY. He hurt her in front of a bunch of kids, like they saw him, a man, backhand a woman in the face and hurt her, / that's –

JOEY. GOD Ray, not on purpose, though, I'm sure it wasn't *malicious* / – it.

RAY. Now I don't know if they will hire him back.

JOEY. Of course they will – He's like an institution at that school. He has all his little disciples who follow him around.

RAY. I'm serious, Joey. They might not and we have to think about that possibility –

JOEY. But they obviously WANT to, that's why they're making him meet with Carver the Strange.

RAY. Stop, he's nice.

JOEY. He's weird, Ray. He has a – weird look in his eyes.

RAY. Well they're just so SAD – I kind of couldn't look away from / them –

JOEY. Yeah they're like a car wreck. You know he's the Father Caldwell kid.

RAY. I know.

JOEY. So…I'm not totally sure he's the best judge of mental health, but whatever –

RAY. He drives by and checks on Dad every night.

JOEY. What?

RAY. Or most nights, I guess, he like, drives by the house and "checks in."

JOEY. Weird.

RAY. …Hey, don't tell Mom, okay?

JOEY. I won't.

RAY. He doesn't want her to know.

JOEY. Yeah, I can see why.

I'm going to swim some laps.

RAY. I thought we were going to swim together.

JOEY. So come with me.

RAY. No – just stay here for a minute.

Did you notice there's nothing in his fridge?

JOEY. I didn't look.

RAY. There used to be so much food when we'd come home.

JOEY. Well he's on a tighter budget now.

RAY. Plus, he just doesn't *look* good, you know? Like I feel like he hasn't had a haircut in – I don't know – and then Carver acted like it was a big deal that he even went out to the store, which makes me think he hasn't been leaving the house at all, to even buy groceries, / so –

JOEY. Ray.

RAY. Do you think I should move back home for a while?

JOEY. What and quit your job working for Maria?

RAY. Ehhh.

JOEY. What?

   (**RAY** *shrugs and looks down.*)

 Ray. No!

RAY. Yeah.

JOEY. Nooo that was really stupid!

RAY. Well I didn't know what else / to do –

JOEY. Ray. Noooooo. That was really shitty of you.

RAY. I'll figure it out.

JOEY. *(Covering her eyes.)* How are you going to pay rent? I'm leaving in less than a month – The subletter's not going to cover you –

RAY. I'll figure it out.

JOEY. We cannot lose that apartment, / Ray.

RAY. I'll talk to Dad about it.

JOEY. Dad's got his own shit to worry about, he can't be helping you pay rent –

RAY. I know, I just –

JOEY. You are such a fucking mess, you know that?

RAY. God Joey.

JOEY. Now I have to worry about this too?!

   (**JOEY** *shakes her head and covers her face.*)

RAY. Joey.

JOEY. *(Inhaling, turning around.)* I'm going to swim laps.

RAY. Joey.

   (**JOEY** *heads toward the water.*)

 Don't go for too long.

 And don't go where I can't see you!

   (**JOEY** *swims away.* **RAY** *sits alone.*)

     ***

6.

(JEAN, BOBBY, and TOM sing and play instruments. RAY sings along here and there. TOM's voice is gravelly and deep and extraordinary in some way. JOEY listens, a little distant from the group, lost in her thoughts, her head leaning on the porch rail.)

TOM.

NOW THE SKY AND STARS AND TREES
SEEM TO SCREAM YOUR NAME
EVER SINCE YOU LEFT ME, LEFT ME ALL ALONE
NOW I SEE YOUR PRETTY FACE
IN EVERY FUCKIN' PLACE
AND IT'S KILLING ME IT'S KILLING ME I KNOW

TOM & BOBBY.

WELL DARLIN' SINCE YOU LEFT ME
HERE I CAN'T FACE MYSELF
I'M CRYING AND I'M LONELY ALL THE TIME
YOUR SMELL IS IN MY BED
AND YOUR WORDS ARE IN MY HEAD
AND I'M DYING HERE I'M DYING HERE INSIDE

TOM, BOBBY, RAY & JEAN.

WELL I TELL YOU
(I TELL YOU HONEY)
I'M CALLING
(ACROSS THE PLAINS)
I'M CALLING OUT YOUR NAME

WELL THE YEARS HAVE COME AND GONE
JUST A SAD PARADE
I SIT MOST NIGHTS ALONE OUT ON THE LAWN
THINKING OF OLD SONGS
AND ALL THAT I DID WRONG
AND PUSHING THROUGH YEAH PUSHING THROUGH TILL
    DAWN

I'M HOPING
(I TELL YOU HONEY)

> YOU HEAR ME
> (ACROSS THE PLAINS)
> I NEVER MEANT TO CAUSE YOU ANY PAIN

TOM & RAY.

> YEAH THE SKY AND STARS AND TREES STILL CRY OUT
>   YOUR NAME
> SINCE YOU LEFT ME, LEFT ME ALONE SO LONG AGO
> AND I STILL SEE YOUR PRETTY FACE
> IN EVERY FUCKIN' PLACE
> AND IT'S KILLING ME, IT'S KILLING ME, I KNOW.

> *(They clap.)*

JEAN. Ooooh I love that one.

BOBBY. Yeah, thats a great one.

RAY. It's depressing as hell though, Dad!

BOBBY. Yep, that's why it's / good.

TOM. All of the good ones are.

JEAN. Your dad's coming along on that guitar, isn't he Ray?

RAY. He is.

TOM. I'm trying.

JEAN. You going to play us something, Miss Ray?

RAY. Mmmm don't know.

BOBBY. Aw, come on. We didn't come all the way over here just to listen to your dad screeching on like he / does.

TOM. Hey now – these two girls were born and raised on my screeching!

JEAN. We want to hear what you've been working on.

RAY. Maybe in a little bit.

BOBBY. You can keep that guitar while you're here.

RAY. Oh no, that's okay – I don't need / to –

JEAN. Girl, keep it – You know we have twelve more at home.

BOBBY. Keep it till you leave. I'll be real pissed at you if you don't.

RAY. *(Laughing.)* Okay, I will…

TOM. Thank you Bob.

RAY. Thanks.

BOBBY. Of course. But I expect a full concert before you go, now.

RAY. *(Laughing it off.)* Oh god, I dont know about that...

JEAN. Ooooooh I am so happy to see you girls. It has been way too long.

RAY. I know.

JEAN. It does us all so much good to have you here, don't it, Tom?

TOM. It does.

JEAN. Like a *much* needed breath of fresh air.

> (**JEAN** *looks at* **TOM**, *then squeezes* **RAY**'s *arm;* **RAY** *smiles and nods, glances at her dad.* **BOBBY** *hums quietly to himself and plucks out a simple song.)*

You're real quiet over there Joey.

JOEY. Oh – yeah.

JEAN. You all right?

JOEY. Yeah yeah, just – listening.

BOBBY. Hey, now – tell us about your fancy fellowship?

JOEY. Oh – yeah – so I'm going to Germany in a few weeks.

BOBBY. Right right. And how long is it, now?

JOEY. About two years.

JEAN. Two years?!

TOM. It's a Fulbright, y'all. That's not just fancy, that's – prestigious as / HELL.

JOEY. Okay.

TOM. She beat the shit out of over a million other brilliant people for it.

BOBBY. I bet she did.

JOEY. That is not true.

TOM. It sure as hell is! I was looking at the website, and there's her name there, like they have this whole thing about her, with an interview and all that, and I'm like, Jesus, that's MY daughter!

JEAN. Well that's just amazing – You'll have to send us some pictures.

BOBBY. Oooh, yes – I'd love to see some pictures.

JOEY. Okay, sure, I can do that.

JEAN. That is just amazing, Jo.

JOEY. Thank you, yeah. I'm excited.

TOM. But it's not surprising, right?! This kid is unstoppable.

*(They laugh. **RAY** looks at her hands.)*

JEAN. This'll be hard on you, huh Ms. Ray? Two years so far away?!

RAY. Yeahhh. Trying not to think about it!

(The girls glance at each other.)

JOEY. *(Yawning.)* Whew. I might have to head to bed soon.

TOM. You need to eat more protein, girl.

JOEY. *(Laughing.)* What?!

TOM. *(To **JEAN** and **BOBBY**.)* She's a vegan now, for some godforsaken / reason.

BOBBY. Oh, no, you're leaving us for the dark side / Joey?!

JEAN. Oh – stop now, shes just being healthy. I admire you for it, girl.

JOEY. Thank you, Jean! And I eat protein Dad.

TOM. Why the hell are you being vegan all of a sudden?

JOEY. Because it's healthier than eating processed meat and dairy that have been injected full of antibiotics and hormones?

TOM. Well watch out, because I'm going to sneak some steak into you when you're not looking.

JOEY. Ew, please don't.

TOM. When you're sleeping later, I'm going to sneak in and put a little piece of ribeye under your tongue.

JOEY. Ew, god!

TOM. I am. You better sleep with one eye open.

JOEY. Gross.

TOM. Aw come on, you used to love steak.

JOEY. I never loved steak. Ray loved it.

TOM. *(Gripping* **RAY***'s shoulder.)* And Ray still loves it. Because Ray is a sane, normal, warm-blooded human being.

JOEY. Whatever.

TOM. Whatever. You better be eating real food over there in Germany.

JOEY. Goodnight Everyone.

BOBBY. Goodnight, hon.

TOM. Eat a hamburger while you're in there!

> *(She shakes her head and disappears inside the house.)*

(To **RAY***.)* How long has this vegan thing been going on?

RAY. *(Shrugging.)* Not that long. A few months?

TOM. I don't like it...

RAY. She's fine.

JEAN. Gol-ly – *Germany!* That is so exciting.

TOM. I know.

JEAN. *(To* **RAY***.)* Two years, huh?

RAY. Yeahhh.

JEAN. When was the last time y'all spent any time apart?

RAY. Uhhhh we haven't really, ever.

BOBBY. Well she can go visit – You can visit, can't you?

RAY. I...yeah, I could. It's expensive.

TOM. Well I'm sure your mom can help foot the bill.

> *(***RAY*** *just looks at him and shakes her head.)*

JEAN. Well, I think you should come stay here with us for awhile. We'd all like that.

RAY. ...Aww, yeah maybe I should!

TOM. The girl's got a job, Jean, she can't be hanging out with us old folks down here...

BOBBY. You still working for that same lady, the uh...?

RAY. Uhhhh, yeah, sort of.

TOM. Sort of?

JEAN. She does what again?

RAY. She runs a foundation. Like they give grants to artists for research and things like / that.

JEAN. That's right, that's right. Right up your alley.

RAY. Yeah.

TOM. What's this you "sort of" work for her?

RAY. I don't know, I – make my own hours, I mean.

JEAN. Oh, that's nice.

BOBBY. Good for a musician.

TOM. But she's still offering you benefits?

RAY. Uhh, sort of, / but –.

TOM. What is this "sort of" crapola?

RAY. DAD – We have something worked out.

TOM. I don't like the sound of this at all.

RAY. You don't like the sound of anything. So…stop, it's fine. Wait, so, how're Bea and Buster?

JEAN. Oh they're crazy as ever. Bea's got some arthritis in her back legs, but she's still doing pretty good for an old lady.

RAY. Awww I miss them.

BOBBY. Well y'all come over while you're here and visit. They love you girls.

RAY. Yeah, we will. Dad, you should get a dog. I think it'd be good for you.

TOM. And why is that?

RAY. You could use the company, and. I think it would be good to have something to take care of.

JEAN. That's right, Tom.

TOM. Y'all all think I'm dying of loneliness or something?

RAY. No, just…

JEAN. It'd be good to have something else to focus on right now. We all think so.

RAY. Yeah.

JEAN. You need to get out of your head, Tommy. You're making yourself sick – obsessing over something that's not gonna change.

RAY. YEAH, Dad – it'd be good for you.

TOM. Ladies: I am doing. Fine. Tell them, Bob, that I'm fine.

BOBBY. *(Laughing, shaking his head.)* Ehhhh I think it's about time you played us a song, Miss Ray. How about it, Miss singer-songwriter?

RAY. Oh, no… I don't really have anything good right now.

BOBBY. Come on…

TOM. Don't hold out on us now.

RAY. I seriously don't have anything.

BOBBY. I don't believe that for a / second.

RAY. No, no, I am unfortunately telling you the truth.

TOM. Don't be scared now, come on.

RAY. I'm not.

TOM. Yes you are, now, let's / hear it.

RAY. I seriously don't have anything.

> *(Quiet.)*

Sorry. I just – Yeah, haven't been doing as much music lately. I think I'm actually gonna try to do something else for awhile…

> *(She looks at her hands and shrugs.)*

So.

> *(She glances at her dad.* **TOM** *shakes his head.)*

TOM. When did you decide that?

RAY. *(Shrugging.)* I don't know, just – recently, I guess.

TOM. *(Shaking his head.)* …You give up too easy, Rayleen.

RAY. What?

TOM. You get scared off too easy and don't like to finish what you start.

RAY. Dad, god – what are you talking / about?

TOM. I'm being serious.

RAY. Okay, well, wow, I'm sorry I'm such a disappointment!

TOM. Baby, I'm just telling you you gotta dig yourself further into things before you just give up on it all!

RAY. You're being a real dick, you know that?

TOM. What'd you say to me?

RAY. I said you're being a dick.

> *(She smirks at him then looks down. A long pause.)*

TOM. *(Quiet.)* ...All I was saying was: You can do better, Rayleen.

> *(They are quiet for a long moment. The crickets purr.)*

JEAN. ...Ooof. Let's burn some sage up in here. I think we should have some of that pie I brought over. Okay, y'all? Let's all eat some pie.

TOM. Yes ma'am. Pie.

RAY. *(Standing.)* I'll get plates.

JEAN. Thanks hon.

> *(She disappears inside, the screen door slamming. **TOM** takes a sip of his drink.)*

Tommy –

TOM. I know, Jean, dammit, I know.

JEAN. All right.

> *(**BOBBY** raises his eyebrows and smiles at **JEAN**, then looks into his guitar. **JEAN** shakes her head. **TOM** wipes his brow, grimacing, then stares out at the yard. The crickets' purring grows.)*

***

7.

(Night. The crickets chirp. **CARVER** *sits in his car, listening to the radio, the* **DJ'S VOICE** *streaming in.)*

LATE NIGHT DJ. – But before I turn in for the night, I'll send you off with the first song from a beautiful brand new album. You heard it here first, kids. This little diamond is from Reservoir, by the Moonlight Miles... And may it both buoy you up and break your heart as it has mine...

*(****CARVER**** glances at the radio, then stares up at the moon. A song streams out into the darkness around him. He sings along to himself, and at some moment, allows himself to remember what it felt like to play music, allows himself to get carried away.)*

COME HOME SOON
MY HEAD IS A BALLOON
AND IT GOES UP UP
HITS THE SURFACE OF MY CUP
HOLD MY CLAVICLE UP
THE ASTEROID BREAKING APART
IN MY FRONT YARD

IT WAS OVER BY JUNE
I THOUGHT I WAS IMMUNE
BUT THE CLOCKWORK CAUGHT
IT WASN'T HOW I THOUGHT
HOLD MY CLAVICLE UP
THE ASTEROID TRIANGULATES
ON THE HOOD OF MY CAR

I'VE BEEN DRINKING ALL NIGHT LONG
I'VE BEEN DRINKING ALL NIGHT
DON'T WANNA TELL YOU 'BOUT WHAT I DID WRONG
DON'T WANNA TELL YOU 'BOUT WHAT I DID WRONG
DON'T WANNA TELL YOU 'BOUT WHAT I DID WRONG

*(****CARVER**** comes back to the present, back to himself.)*

***

PART II

8.

(Late, late that night. **JOEY** *climbs up the rocks from the reservoir, dripping. She pulls her running shorts on over her wet skin when she hears* **TED** *approach.)*

TED. Oh – Hello.

JOEY. *(Startled.)* Hi.

TED. I'm sorry, I –

JOEY. No no, you're fine.

> *(He looks away. She pulls her T-shirt on over her sports bra.)*

TED. I apologize.

JOEY. Don't – no need.

TED. I didn't think I'd run into anyone at this hour.

JOEY. ...Surprise.

TED. I'm sorry if I startled you.

JOEY. No, no it's – okay.

TED. Are you a night swimmer?

JOEY. Not usually, no.

TED. / Ah.

JOEY. Are you?

TED. No, no – just an insomniac.

> *(She nods. He stares up at the moon.)*

JOEY. I know you.

TED. You do?

JOEY. You're a poet.

TED. Yes. How did / you –

JOEY. You were a Visiting Artist over at St. Nick's – when I was a senior. You did a reading.

TED. Oh, wow, that was –

JOEY. Years ago, yeah. Are you teaching at the college now?

TED. Yes, I – well, they hired my wife first, but were willing to take me on as part of a package deal, so...

JOEY. Ahhhh, okay. I loved that reading.

TED. Oh god, really?

JOEY. Yeah. It was – It made a real impression – I mean, I seriously still think about one of those poems.

TED. Good god, well – you might be the only person –

JOEY. Yeah, it was –. Yeah, it was about this hotel room in a foreign city, and the guy is there, sitting on the bed, kind of feeling alone, and looking out the window of the balcony. And his wife or – girlfriend or whoever is in the bath, and she gets out of the bath and comes up behind him, and the steam from her body fogs up the window, and he says, like – "And I almost loved you."

TED. Ha. Right.

JOEY. That whole image, just – yeah, made a deep impression on me. Or taught me about longing?

TED. Wow, well...yeah. Thank you. That's an old poem.

JOEY. Do you hate it now?

TED. Ohhhh, it's like looking at a picture of yourself from middle school.

JOEY. Right.

TED. With all your – braces and bad skin. I guess there are a few, that are somehow able to escape that whole making-you-want-to-shoot-yourself – / thing –

JOEY. Right. They escape time somehow.

TED. I guess so.

JOEY. Because they're truly great.

TED. Is that what it is?

JOEY. Yes.

TED. Hm.

I'm sorry – I'm Ted.

JOEY. Ted? I thought it was "Theodore."

TED. Just Ted to my – well, you're probably too young to be a peer, but... Ted.

JOEY. *(Holding out her hand.)* Joey.

TED. Joey?

JOEY. Josephine, really, but – Joey.

TED. Ahh, okay. It's nice to meet you, Joey.

JOEY. And you.

(Gesturing to the water.)

So are you out here looking for inspiration?

TED. I – God, I'm not. I probably should be? I'm just... walking.

JOEY. You don't find this reservoir deeply inspiring?

TED. *(Laughing.)* I...

JOEY. It's okay, I know it's not.

TED. No no, it is...in its own murky way.

JOEY. Mmkay, well. You've got the Cheshire Cat at least.

TED. Sorry?

JOEY. *(Pointing to the moon.)* The Cheshire Cat is out tonight.

TED. Ahhhh I see, okay okay.

I call that a fingernail clipping moon.

JOEY. A fingernail clipping?

TED. *(Laughing.)* Yes!

JOEY. And I thought you were a fucking poet, sir.

TED. *(Laughing.)* I thought so too – so / – hmm...

JOEY. The Cheshire Cat is quite obviously so much better than a fingernail. He's also the best character in the book.

TED. What about the caterpillar?

JOEY. The *caterpillar* is high as a kite on opium the whole time.

TED. True.

JOEY. You can't trust a thing he says.

TED. But you can trust a cat?

JOEY. I didn't say that. But no one's better than the Cheshire Cat. He creeps down at you when you're not looking.

(She grins.)

TED. ...Yes.

JOEY. So what are you writing about?

TED. Uhhh...

JOEY. I mean are you working on something right now, and if so, what is it?

TED. Oh good god, um –

JOEY. You don't have to say if you don't want. That was a shit question. You can just tell me to fuck off.

TED. No, no – I am just. Not sure how to answer.

JOEY. Fair enough.

Next question –

(She mimes pushing a microphone in his face.)

Ted – How long have you been teaching at the college?

TED. I uh...

(She pushes the imaginary microphone closer; he laughs.)

I... It's been...a year now?

JOEY. *(Turning the mic on herself.)* Oh, so you're still new in town?

TED. *(Into the mic.)* I suppose so?

JOEY. *(Into the mic.)* But it feels like you've been here a lifetime?

TED. *(Laughing.)* I guess I wasn't sure we would end up staying?

JOEY. *(Into the mic.)* Because it's a tiny, tiny-ass town in the middle of fucking nowhere?

TED. Uhhh...

(She thrusts the fake mic at him; he laughs.)

...Yes.

JOEY. *(Into the mic.)* Yes, gotcha, gotcha. And does your wife like it here?

TED. *(Into the mic.)* She does, actually. I honestly thought she might be bored to death after one semester, but –

JOEY. *(Into the mic.)* She's not?

TED. *(Into the mic.)* No. She finds it peaceful. But she's also been able to escape on a book tour, / so.

JOEY. *(Into the mic.)* Ahhhh, I see. She's a poet as well?

TED. *(Into the mic.)* No – A novelist. A brilliant one at that.

JOEY. *(Into the mic.)* Ah – Very nice. A book tour – so she's pretty successful then?

TED. *(Into the mic.)* Yes.

> *(She holds the fake mic there, waiting for him to elaborate. He doesn't.)*

JOEY. Okay – Hey, Ted, thanks for the interview.

TED. You're welcome.

> *(She lets the imaginary mic go.)*

JOEY. Do you hate teaching here?

TED. No, no. The student body is a little...homogeneous, I guess, but –.

JOEY. Yeahh, that's why our mom made us go somewhere else for college.

TED. Us?

JOEY. I have a twin.

TED. Do you?

JOEY. I do

TED. Wow.

JOEY. What?

TED. Twins are still just...so – I can't wrap my mind around it. It's crazy. It's crazy that there are two people who look exactly alike walking around in the world together.

JOEY. Well, we're fraternal so we don't look alike AT ALL.

TED. Oh. Well, sure, / of course not, but –

JOEY. We're quite different actually.

TED. How so?

JOEY. Well, she's a lesbian, to start.

TED. *(Laughing.)* Ah, okay!

JOEY. And I like to run.

TED. And she doesn't.

JOEY. She really doesn't.

TED. I see.

JOEY. And she's a musician and is all creative and messy and all that...

TED. Huh. Well, we just met, but I must say – you, too, seem awfully creative –

JOEY. No no, not like she is. I'm much more type-A, nerdy academic girl. I'm leaving on a Fulbright soon, actually.

TED. Oh – my god. What an honor. Congratulations.

JOEY. Yeah, thank you. Off to Berlin.

TED. Wow.

JOEY. City of...old terrors? Walls? Nazis?

TED. When do you go?

JOEY. A few weeks. So we're just here visiting my dad before we – before I leave.

> *(She gives a quick smile, then exhales, looking down at the water. He looks at the moon, then glances at her.)*

TED. I am actually working on something.

JOEY. Yeah?

TED. To your earlier question. Yes.

JOEY. About?

TED. It's about...a knife.

JOEY. A knife.

TED. Well, being – threatened with a knife.

JOEY. Oh shit – Is it based on real life?

TED. *(Laughing.)* It is, yes.

JOEY. When? – Or, I mean, who threatened / you?

TED. A long time ago. Uhh, my wife did. Actually.

JOEY. Yikes.

TED. Yeah, back when we – before we were married. We used to have these very, sort of – well, violent fights.

JOEY. Ahh, okay.

TED. Emotionally violent, I mean. Loud, explosive. And this time with the knife – We were standing in our tiny, terrible kitchen and...I remember I was so immensely angry, just, truly seething red livid, but I can't...yeah, for the life of me conjure up anything close to that feeling or really remember how I felt that so intensely... So. I'm trying to work on it, but...not getting terribly far.

JOEY. Hmm. I was also once threatened with a knife.

TED. Really?

JOEY. Yeah, I was walking home at night and a guy followed me into the entryway to our building.

TED. Oh no.

JOEY. Yeahhh, he put the knife up to my throat, here, and... yeah, took my wallet and phone and whatever else I had on me. And I got a lot of very exciting bruises.

TED. God, I'm sorry.

JOEY. Yeahhh, it's fun being a girl. Especially these days.

TED. ...Right.

(She raises her eyebrows and then looks away for a moment.)

JOEY. ...But, uh...yeah, I guess the thing I remember about it is...how I was so stuck in this notion that the thing that was happening couldn't possibly be happening – because I was just walking home being a nice person. And then that feeling later shifted into this kind of... clarity about how stupidly, stupidly fragile everything was. That I could have all these hopes and thoughts and just be walking around being, I don't know, a person with a lot of grand hopes and thoughts, and then just get knifed to death by some guy on crack in the entryway to our shitty building in Queens. It was so...well, unpoetic.

TED. Oh, I don't know. There's some poetry in that somewhere.

JOEY. Okay, maybe so.

> *(She laughs.)*

Anyway, I'm sure none of that is helpful to you at ALL!

TED. No no, it is.

JOEY. Oh, well good! – Now you have to credit me whenever the thing gets published.

TED. Right, I will. Whenever that is.

JOEY. Don't sound so bleak.

TED. *(Laughing.)* I feel a little bleak, Joey!

JOEY. Listen, if I'm still thinking about some old poem from a zillion years ago that I heard when I was seventeen and barely a conscious being, then you should absolutely not feel bleak.

TED. And why is that?

JOEY. Because clearly you are capable of truly great, ageless, time-defying stuff.

TED. *(Laughing, rubbing his face.)* Aughhhh I'd like to think that, / but...

JOEY. You are.

TED. Well – thank you, total stranger, for believing in me.

JOEY. Hey, of course.

> *(He looks at her. Then they both look at the moon. They are quiet.* **JOEY** *squints.)*

Is your wife very beautiful?

TED. Uhhhh... She is. Yes.

JOEY. Even by our insane and commercial standards of beauty?

TED. ...I would say so.

JOEY. Yeahhh.

TED. What?

JOEY. Ohhh, it's just disappointing.

TED. Is it?

JOEY. Oh, yes.

TED. I'm not sure why.

JOEY. Well, then you're not terribly intuitive or observant, are you?

TED. *(Laughing.)* God, I – yeah, I guess that could be true.

JOEY. No no, I'm just – fucking with you.

> *(She looks away. He looks at her.)*

TED. I find I...like beautiful things. I'm drawn to them.

JOEY. ...Sure.

> *(She nods at him, then looks away. A long silence.)*

Well – Good luck on your poem.

TED. ...Thank you.

JOEY. Watch out for the Cheshire Cat.

TED. I – yes, I will.

JOEY. Goodnight.

TED. Goodnight.

> *(She turns away, disappearing into the woods. He watches her go, then looks up at the moon.)*

***

9.

(Late morning the next day. **RAY** *sits on the porch, clouded, staring down into Bobby's guitar.* **CARVER** *approaches.)*

CARVER. Hey there.

RAY. Oh! – Hey.

CARVER. You lose something in there?

RAY. What's that?

CARVER. You're staring down in there, / like –

RAY. Oh – no no.

CARVER. Like you lost something.

RAY. No, no, I'm just – pining and – slowly going insane, / so.

CARVER. Pining?

RAY. I'm kidding.

He's in a *great* mood by the way.

CARVER. Oh yeah?

RAY. Just to warn you.

CARVER. *(Laughing.)* Oooh… Okay, thank you.

Hey – probably when you're off doing something else, it'll hit you.

RAY. What?

CARVER. The song.

RAY. Oh – yeah.

CARVER. At least that was how it used to work for me. Anyway – good to see you.

> *(**CARVER** goes inside to where **TOM** sits at the kitchen table, bent over a book, turning a pencil around and around in his hand.)*

Hey there Tom.

TOM. *(Looking up.)* Hey there.

CARVER. How's it going?

TOM. Good, good. Just – reading this fucking terrible book the headmaster wants everyone to read.

CARVER. I see.

TOM. Aren't you proud?

CARVER. Yep, very proud.

TOM. *(Closing the book, rubbing his eyes.)* I'm sorry I missed you the other day. I thought I had rescheduled.

CARVER. Not a problem.

> *(He sits down across from* **TOM.** **TOM** *is silent.* **CARVER** *peers at him kindly.)*

Hey, so I heard you made a trip to the Piggly Wiggly.

TOM. Yup.

CARVER. That's really great, Tom.

TOM. Yeah, isn't it, though? I'm making such progress!

CARVER. You are.

TOM. *(Clamping his hands to his eyes.)* God.

CARVER. How'd it go?

TOM. Ohhhh let's see – it was just lovely. I've so missed all the eyes of this town boring into my skin and willing me to drop dead, so, yeah, no, it was just so – rewarding to be out in public again.

CARVER. What happened?

TOM. Well, lord... I'd say the *highlight* of the whole trip was running smack into the headmaster while he was picking out steaks.

CARVER. Ah.

TOM. And we just had such a good talk.

CARVER. What did you talk about?

TOM. Oh, you know, he was just full of his usual smarmy-ass-I-love-everyone good fucking cheer and he let me know that he's been praying for me, the whole family has been praying for me, and he really does hope "they can have me back."

CARVER. You don't think he was being sincere?

TOM. God, I don't know, he's such a slippery little maggot, I don't know! He said, "Well, hey now, if we bring you back I have some great suggestions on how to improve your syllabus!" And I just stared at the man and couldn't say a damn thing – I mean, I can't even imagine what ridiculous, idiot dreck he thinks my kids should be reading – not to mention, good fucking god – Abstinence?

(He picks up the book.)

Really? They're teenagers! – The more you tell them NOT to do something, the more they will desperately claw their way to do it. Probably unsafely and in total and complete ignorance, because no sane adult has reached out to tell them the truth. And I'll tell you right now, if some – if any of my students turn to me for help on this stuff, I cannot lie to them, I cannot spout off this abstinence bullshit, I just can't.

CARVER. Okay.

TOM. Okay? Are you agreeing with me or not?

CARVER. It doesn't really matter if I agree with / you or not.

TOM. Oh Good Christ!

CARVER. Was Katie there too?

TOM. No, god – thank god.

CARVER. Did you talk about her?

TOM. Well he of course made sure to let me know she's been taking time away to "heal."

CARVER. And what did you say to that?

TOM. I don't know. I don't know! Something completely asinine like, "Well give her my regards," or some idiot shit...

CARVER. That doesn't sound asinine to me, Tom.

TOM. Euughhh.

CARVER. I think it's good you had to see him. It's good to have to – face it. And to see that it wasn't that bad –

TOM. Oh god Carver, no – it was fucking awful. Because I feel fucking awful. All the time. I never stop feeling fucking awful, so –.

(**TOM** shakes his head over and over, his face bare and sad for a moment, his eyes softening.)

I mean, I have daughters, I – and I hurt that woman. I really hurt her.

CARVER. But you didn't mean to.

TOM. And all those kids saw it.

CARVER. You didn't mean to hurt her, Tom.

TOM. You should've seen how those kids were looking at me...

CARVER. She was just in the wrong place at the wrong moment.

TOM. I don't know, I was so angry, I just wanted to strangle somebody, I wanted to – *augh* –. And this is why Meg left the way she did, you know, this is what she said to me and now I'm thinking it's true, it's...

CARVER. What?

TOM. I've become an angry, hateful, old dick.
Everyone thinks it. My own kids think it.

> (*He covers his face.* **CARVER** *stares at him, then reaches for one of his hands.*)

CARVER. Tom.

> (**TOM** *shakes his head.*)

Tom.

> (**CARVER** *pries one of* **TOM**'s *hands away. He holds it.*)

TOM. I have never looked at you and seen anything but your immense kindness.

> (**TOM** *shakes his head.* **CARVER** *stares at him, his face bare and vulnerable for a moment, full of love. Then slowly, slowly,* **TOM** *looks up at* **CARVER**, *watches* **CARVER** *watching him. A long moment. Then* **TOM** *slowly pulls his hand away.*)

Patrick.

CARVER. ...What?

TOM. Son.
What are you doing?

CARVER. I'm sorry?

TOM. Oh no no no.

CARVER. I don't know what you're / asking.

TOM. No no no no.

CARVER. What?

TOM. Oh god, I'm sorry, I've been an idiot. I've been a real idiot.

> *(He looks at his shoes for a moment, squinting.)*

You should go, Carver.

CARVER. No, now – Tom. We need to finish our session.

TOM. I think you should go, son.

CARVER. I think there's been a misunderstanding –

TOM. And we should meet somewhere else from now on, okay?

CARVER. Tom.

TOM. You email me some available times and we'll meet in your office next week, okay?

CARVER. *(Shaking his head.)* ...Okay. I don't – Can we just stop for a second and let me – I think there's a misunderstanding / here –

TOM. You should go son.

CARVER. Tom.

TOM. Go on now.

CARVER. I don't –.

> *(He looks at TOM, then looks down.)*

Excuse me.

> *(CARVER turns to go, leaving TOM behind in the kitchen, one hand over his head. CARVER strides past RAY, who is humming forlornly to herself.)*

RAY. Whoa – Hey, are you going already?

CARVER. Yeah – Good seeing you again.

RAY. *(Half-waving.)* Okay... See ya.

(**CARVER** *disappears.* **RAY** *watches him go, then goes into the kitchen, where* **TOM** *stands with his back to her.*)

What happened?

TOM. Nothing.

RAY. Well he tore out of here like something did.

TOM. Just – stay out of it Ray, would you?

RAY. Dad.

TOM. Stay out of it, I said.

(*He looks at her, then away. She looks at him.*)

Were you working on something out there?

RAY. Nope.

TOM. (*Grabbing the guitar from her hand.*) Well here, let me see that thing.

WELL IT'S A COUNTRY SONG
EVERYTHING GOES WRONG.
YEAH IT ALL GOES WRONG
IT'S A COUNTRY SONG
YOU FUCK IT UP IN THE END...

Remember that one? Might be the best one you ever wrote...

RAY. Might be.

TOM.

OHH IT'S A COUNTRY SONG
IT ALL GOES FUCKING WRONG
EVERYTHING GOES WRONG
IN A COUNTRY SONG
IT'S ALL SHIT BY THE END.
COME ON MISS RAY!

RAY. No thanks.

TOM. No?

RAY. Nope.

(*He stops playing. He looks around.*)

TOM. Now where'd Joey get to?

RAY. Running.

TOM. *(Shaking his head.)* Lord. That girl.
I'm worried about her.

RAY. Yeah.

> *(She looks up at him for a moment, then heads back outside.)*

TOM. Going out?

RAY. Yup.

> *(She disappears. He looks after her, then looks around the kitchen. He closes his eyes for a moment, then opens them again, weary.)*

***

10.

(The reservoir; night. **JOEY** *is climbing back up the rocks;* **TED** *appears, staring down at her.)*

TED. Hello down there!

JOEY. Hello!

TED. Are you going in?

JOEY. *(Climbing up.)* What's that?

TED. You're not going in?

JOEY. Oh, no, no swimming for me tonight.

TED. No?

JOEY. No.

TED. Just staring off into the distance?

JOEY. *(Laughing.)* Yeahhh, just – thinking.

TED. Thinking. Okay. About what?

JOEY. Ohh. You know.

TED. I don't.

JOEY. Just –. The future.

TED. What about it?

JOEY. Oh, you know, just...how huge and gaping of an unknown hole it is.

TED. *(Laughing.)* Good god, okay.

JOEY. You asked.

TED. I did.

JOEY. Did you finish your poem?

TED. Uhhhhhh – no.

JOEY. Ohh, so you're here to seek more of my wisdom and insight?

TED. *(Laughing.)* I suppose so, maybe, yes.

JOEY. We could do some role-playing.

TED. Sorry?

JOEY. For inspiration.

TED. All right, I'll...yeah, let you know if I need / that –

JOEY. Great, yeah, just say the word and I'll knife you.

TED. *(Laughing.)* Oh god.

Okay, I will.

Why is the future such a gaping black hole?

JOEY. Ohhhhhh I am going to Berlin.

TED. Yes.

JOEY. Alone.

TED. Sure.

JOEY. I don't know anyone, no one knows me, and I don't know what it will be, / so.

TED. Right...but won't it be nice to be anonymous for awhile? A stranger in a strange city?

JOEY. Maybe.

TED. I mean it – I think it's so useful to be able to just – disappear. Like that.

JOEY. Yeah...hm.

TED. Why Berlin, by the way?

JOEY. Ohhh the darkness of it appealed to me, I guess.

TED. Okay.

JOEY. I like that...it has all these old, terrible scars – like there's this old wound that won't go away and you can still sort of see where the stitches were... So, that appealed to me. Also we were obsessed with *Cabaret* when we were little, so...

TED. Oh, so you just want to be Sally Bowles.

JOEY. Well, sure. I'd like to go out in a burst of flames.

TED. Right.

JOEY. But, yeah... Now the whole – thing is just looming over me in this awful way, so...blah blah blah.

(She shakes it off, then looks up at the moon.)

But how are you?

TED. I'm. Uhhhhhh – oh, you know. Sleepless and restless and bored and full of self-loathing.

JOEY. *(Pretending to leave.)* Oh, okay, well, cool – Hey, GREAT seeing you!

TED. *(Laughing.)* Okay, bye!

JOEY. *(Waving.)* Good luck with everything!

TED. Oh, thanks – yeah!

JOEY. Have a great life!

TED. Thank you!

JOEY. No – no, I mean, I get being bored and restless and the self-hatred part, but why can't you sleep?!

TED. *(Laughing.)* I don't know! I don't know. Suzanne's on this book tour, and I / am just...

JOEY. Oh, right right.

TED. Not. I am not on a book tour.

JOEY. Right.

TED. I am staring at the same poem I've been staring at for months upon months, and I can just – I can just *hear* her being out in the world being prolific and productive, so... And not just *her*, I mean, but everyone. I can hear every other person out there typing and typing away at the most brilliant, wonderful stuff...and it's all echoing together in the most terrific, thundering sound, and – yeah, keeping me awake.

JOEY. *(Nodding.)* Hmm. Well, if it's any consolation, I can't sleep either.

TED. Restless and bored?

JOEY. Oh, well, sure *that*, but...

No... I had a visit from the Cheshire Cat.

TED. *(Laughing.)* Did you?

JOEY. Last night. I did.

TED. And what did he say?

JOEY. Heee said. Well. I was sitting in the kitchen, trying to read an article about East German literature and the demise of the socialist Utopia and just feeling – you know – inadequate and unprepared and terrible, so.

TED. So.

JOEY. So I got up and went over to the kitchen sink, and stared into the glare of the moon, which I realized at that moment was very bright, sort of eerily bright, actually. Like it really was a strong sort of beam of light just – yeah, just thrusting itself through the window and into a little pool on the linoleum. So I stepped into it, and closed my eyes, and felt this – well, this kind of intense, yellow-white light on my face, just standing there for a moment in it, kind of warmed by it, and then I opened my eyes, and there he was.

TED. The cat?

JOEY. Well – a face. I couldn't yet tell what it belonged to.

TED. Yikes.

JOEY. Yeah, just – a face. Kind of framed in the woods, there. So I stood there for a moment, looking at him. And he looked back at me. And it was funny, I had thought the light was coming from the moon, but it wasn't. It was coming from his teeth.

TED. *(Watching her.)* Huh.

JOEY. So I went outside and walked out into the lawn, halfway to the woods, with the light from his teeth illuminating me in this sort of spotlight, and I stood on the lawn and I said, "Hello there." And his eyes were yellow, you know that animal kind of yellow? And he said, "You ought to go further into the woods." And I said, "What?" And he said, "You ought to go deeper into the woods." "Why?" I said. And he said, "You never walk far enough in – you always just stand on the edge and peer in, and then get frightened and pull back. But you ought to go further in." "But I don't know what I might find in there," I said. And he said, "It will be very dark, and wet, too dark to see for awhile, and you will have to feel your way through, and there will be the strange hum of the trees all around you, and your feet will fall through holes in the dead leaves and slithering things may brush past your arm, and all the branches of all the trees will reach out and touch your face, but if you let them, and you keep going blindly like that for awhile, your eyes will adjust." And then, he said...

TED. *(Quiet.)* ...What?

JOEY. "Then you will see all kinds of things. Things that are born and that die only in the deepest part of the woods. Things you could never see otherwise. Truly beautiful things. You ought to go further in," he said.
And then he grinned.

(**TED** *stares at her, rapt.*)

TED. And then what happened?

JOEY. Then I went to bed.

TED. How could you sleep after that?

JOEY. Well it's very exhausting talking to a cat. Plus it was almost four a.m.

(*She gives a small grin. He shakes his head.*)

TED. You are...

JOEY. What?

TED. A strange and beautiful creature.

JOEY. Oh. Well. All I'm saying is maybe you should go further into the woods.

TED. Maybe so.

(*A pause. They look at each other.* **JOEY** *shivers and laughs.*)

JOEY. Whew I think I creeped myself out just now.

TED. Oh no.

JOEY. I'm going to freak out running home in the dark.

TED. Oh no.

JOEY. I might have a panic attack.

TED. Well don't do that.

JOEY. Well, I'll try not to, but...woo –

(*She laughs/gasps.*)

– my heart's going.

(*She laughs nervously.*)

TED. Here.

JOEY. What?

(He scoots closer to her and places his hand on her chest, below her neck, just above her breasts.)

JOEY. What's that supposed / to do?

TED. Shhhh, just. Breathe into my hand.

JOEY. What.

TED. Just breathe into it.

JOEY. Just – like –

TED. Yeah.

JOEY. I'm.

TED. Just.

(She closes her eyes and breathes for a few moments, quiet, into the warmth of his palm. She laughs.)

What?

JOEY. ...I am so afraid.

(She laughs again. Then her face goes bare, vulnerable. They look at each other.)

***

PART III

11.

(Night. A week later. **CARVER** *sits in his car, his eyes tired, a little stricken, a little delirious, sweating. He turns on the radio; the* **DJ'S VOICE** *streams in.)*

LATE NIGHT DJ. – And here's my favorite off of what's surely going to go down as one of the year's most perfect albums. This is one of those songs you just want to hear over and over and over again, you won't ever seem to get tired of it even though it makes you ache with loneliness, even though it just about kills you...

(A strange tone rises underneath the **DJ'S VOICE.***)*

...and if you're like me, you'll think about that place you came from, that kid you once were, scribbling lyrics down in your little notebook, fancying yourself an artist, the world stretching out in front of you in the way it seemed like it was going to, and you'll think about all those things you used to feel, that person you used to be, but then remember you gotta tuck that away –

CARVER. Fold it up small, like a piece of paper –

LATE NIGHT DJ. Over and over, end to end.

CARVER. Till it's real tiny, till you don't ever have to look at it.

LATE NIGHT DJ. Till no one can see any evidence of it anymore. So! Here you go, my night owls, a new and timeless song by the Moonlight Miles...

(The song streams out of the radio.)

RADIO.

THE STREET IS LIT ALONE
BY A SINGLE BULB HANGING FROM A WIRE
THE TOWN THAT WE ALL KNOW
IT'S STILL OUT THERE
IT'S STILL ON FIRE
WE'LL NEVER GO HOME

THERE WAS ONCE A LIGHT INSIDE
SOMEONE'S EYE
EYE
IT WAS BRIGHT, IT SHONE A TIME
I SWEAR I SAW IT, IT WAS MINE

NOT ALL HAD THIS LUCK
NOT ALL SWAM ENOUGH AWAY FROM THE SHIP
SOME ARE STILL BELOW
WITH THE WRECKAGE
DO THEY KNOW
DO THEY KNOW? (WHERE THEY ARE?)

THERE WAS ONCE A LIGHT INSIDE
SOMEONE'S EYE
EYE
IT WAS BRIGHT, IT SHONE A TIME
I SWEAR I SAW IT, IT WAS MINE

*(**CARVER** stares up at the moon, rubbing his eyes.)*

***

12.

(The reservoir; later that night. **JOEY** *and* **TED** *climb back onto the rocks, dripping. There is a small heaviness to* **TED,** *but* **JOEY** *is laughing, buoyant. She grips her chest and laughs.)*

JOEY. *(Laughing.)* AUUUUGHHHHHH!

TED. *(Trying to laugh.)* What?

JOEY. Oh god, I just – feel this thing!

TED. What's that?

JOEY. Just this –

(She gestures.)

– you know?!

TED. I...do, I / think –

JOEY. That – the world feels huge and open and there's this – yeah, this churning, swelling – sea of a feeling – you know?

TED. *(Nodding quietly.)* I...think that's youth you're / feeling.

JOEY. Like I just feel – *FREE* – from *everythiiiiiiiiiiiiiii iiiiiiiiiiiiiing*!

(She turns to him, her face glowing and alive.)

Do you want to go somewhere?

TED. What?

JOEY. Like drive somewhere?

TED. Where?

JOEY. I don't care, I don't care – Let's just drive somewhere.

TED. Wow, well –

JOEY. We can just drive through the night and the next day and then stay over in some crap hotel and eat continental breakfast?!

TED. *(Laughing.)* That – I would love to do that.

JOEY. Can we take your car?

TED. You're serious.

JOEY. Yes! Can we?

TED. I – We could.

JOEY. Okay.

TED. I would really like to.

JOEY. Okay...

TED. But I can't.

JOEY. Why?

TED. ...Suzanne's coming home

JOEY. ...Ah.

TED. She cancelled her stop in Atlanta, so she's coming home early.

JOEY. Oh.

TED. So. Though you are completely intoxicating, I can't / –.

JOEY. Of course. Yeah.

TED. Even though I've come to...even though these nights have been so – lovely. I don't want anything to get tangled and ugly and and and –.

JOEY. Sure. No one wants that.

TED. Maybe this is – I don't know, I wonder if we could consider it a kind of brief and wonderful...like a tiny piece of time that's somehow outside of regular time?

JOEY. *(Nodding.)* Right.

TED. At least I'd like to think of it that way.

> *(They stand there, silent for a moment.* **JOEY** *pulls her T-shirt on over wet skin. She holds up her pretend microphone, weakly)*

JOEY. Well, Theodore, it's been so fun talking to you.

> *(She thrusts her fake mic toward his face.)*

TED. It has.

JOEY. *(Into her mic.)* Out here in the woods.

> *(She thrusts it back at him.)*

TED. ...Yes.

JOEY. *(Into her mic.)* Where things are born and then they die and no one ever knows they were there.

> *(She grins at him, then drops the game.)*

TED. There are a lot of wonderful things ahead for you, I hope you know that.

JOEY. Ehhhhhh well right now I just feel like a fucking idiot, so...

TED. Please don't.

JOEY. *(Shrugging, staring at her feet.)* Eh.

TED. Let me walk you home.

JOEY. Nah, I'm good.

TED. It's late, Joey – let me walk you.

JOEY. I'm good. I'd prefer to run.

TED. I'd really like to walk you.

JOEY. Well we can't have all things, can we.

TED. Joey.

JOEY. You should go. Really.

> **(TED** *looks at her; she looks at the ground.)*

Please go.

TED. ...Okay.

> **(TED** *slowly steps away, then disappears into the woods.* **JOEY** *looks after him, then down at her feet, running her foot along the rock. She looks up at the moon. She puts a hand to her chest, breathing, vulnerable, muttering "fuck fuck fuck" to herself. She turns and sprints away, disappearing into the darkness.)*

***

13.

(Before dawn, the living room. **RAY** *stares into the glow of her phone.* **TOM** *appears from the bedroom.)*

TOM. Where's your sister?

RAY. What?

TOM. She isn't here.

RAY. She snuck out.

TOM. What? – Where?

RAY. I don't know! Running?

TOM. In the middle of the night?

RAY. You know she's insane, she goes out every night and probably runs an Ironman up the mountain or / something.

TOM. It's not funny, Ray.

RAY. I'm not being funny, she's seriously been sneaking out every night.

TOM. Well why haven't you stopped her?

RAY. I don't know.

TOM. *(Looking outside.)* You're supposed to stop her, Ray!

RAY. I'm sorry! / I'm sorry.

TOM. Goddamnit. That girl. Goddamnit.

(He peers outside.)

RAY. Hey, I know I'm not out running marathons at four in the morning, but I'm also not doing that great.

TOM. What?

RAY. In case you care.

TOM. Of course I care, baby, I'm – what's – what?

RAY. Uhhhhhh well let's see...I can't stop Joey. And I can't write a song for shit and I don't even know if I want to / anymore –

TOM. Okay, now –

RAY. Aaaaand I've been sleeping with my boss, who is literally twenty years older than me, so – there's that.

TOM. Wait, now – wait. Who / is this?

RAY. My boss.

TOM. The woman?

RAY. Yes. The woman.

...So I quit. Because I thought we shouldn't be "together" and also work together, like I thought that would make it easier for her, but it's been – radio silence. On that. So I basically just – Yeah, that hurts so much I want to curl up and die –

TOM. Okay –

RAY. – And Joey's imploding and you're – hitting women – in the face – and I don't know if I should move back home or what I should do about any of it, so –. / Yeah.

TOM. But this... / okay.

RAY. But whatever.

TOM. ...This woman, now...you love her?

RAY. *(Her eyes filling.)* ...Yeah.

TOM. And she...loves you?

RAY. *(Laughing/crying.)* I don't know! I thought so, but...

TOM. Does she respect you?

RAY. *(Wiping her face.)* I mean...I think so.

TOM. You think so?

RAY. I / don't know –

TOM. This doesn't sound good, Rayleen.

RAY. I know! I know, but – I don't know, I'm – She's loud and funny and just – luminous – so. I know it's not, or it wasn't a *smart* thing to do, I know / that, but –

TOM. Sure, but the smart things are not always so fun.

RAY. Yeah, but...

Not feeling so fun anymore.

Anyway.

TOM. *(Peering at her.)* Well now I'm worried about both of y'all girls.

RAY. Well I'm worried about you, Dad. I'm really worried.

TOM. Well that's not your job.

RAY. It is, though, Dad. It's – that's our job now.

TOM. *(Shaking his head.)* Euuughh but I hate that.

RAY. I know.

> *(They look at each other.* **TOM** *holds* **RAY***'s shoulder and squeezes it.)*
>
> *(The phone rings.)*

***

PART IV

14.

(**TOM** *sits with* **JOEY** *in the living room. She sleeps.* **CARVER** *stands over by the doorway.*)

CARVER. ...Hey, Tom, I, / uh –

TOM. Yeah – hey.

CARVER. I thought I'd head out unless you need me / to –

TOM. Oh god, of course – no – you don't need to stay.

CARVER. Okay.

> (*He looks out toward the yard, then back at* **TOM,** *who is staring, stricken, at* **JOEY.**)

The nurse was saying she might sleep for awhile. Partly 'cause of whatever they gave her.

TOM. (*Quiet. He laughs to himself and rubs his face.*) She was always such a shitty sleeper.

CARVER. Yeah?

TOM. God yes. Kept me up at all hours. Ray would sleep nine, ten hours straight, but not Joey.
I'd walk her around and around and we'd stand at the back door and watch the raccoons dig through the neighbors' trash and I'd sing her a song...

> (*He laughs, shaking his head.*)

Auughhh, it's funny, you–. I don't think I knew what fear was till the girls came along.

CARVER. Right.

TOM. So, um – Thank you, Carver, for finding her.

CARVER. Oh, well... I'm just glad I was out driving.

TOM. Me too, or she'd've been lying there all night.

(CARVER smiles at TOM and shakes his head. RAY appears next to him, coming in from the porch, holding her phone.)

RAY. Mom's going to come.

TOM. She doesn't need to do that.

RAY. She wants to.

TOM. She's definitely coming?

RAY. Yeah.

TOM. All right, well.

(He closes his eyes for a moment, inhaling.)

Okay.

(He opens them again, peering at her, unsteady on her feet.)

Ray, honey – why don't you run out and pick up some groceries for us?

RAY. I should be here when she wakes up, / though.

CARVER. Or I can do that for y'all.

TOM. S'gonna be awhile, though, baby, and it'd be good if you could pick up some Gatorade for her.
Carver, son, would you mind going with her?

RAY. I'm fine on / my own.

CARVER. Of course.

TOM. Just – go with Carver, all right? He'll go with you.

CARVER. Happy to.

(RAY hovers in the doorway.)

TOM. Ray?

RAY. Yeah.

TOM. Go on. We'll be fine.

(CARVER puts a hand on her shoulder.)

CARVER. *(To TOM.)* We'll be back soon.

TOM. *(To CARVER.)* Thank you.

(He nods at TOM, TOM nods back. CARVER and RAY head outside.)

(**TOM** *exhales and rubs his hands over his face, lost, terrified.*)

(**TOM** *holds* **JOEY**'s *hand and sings* "The Raccoon Song.")

BIRDS LIVE ON THE DOOR
POSSUMS IN THE FLOOR
CHEWING ON THEIR PAWS
LITTLE HANDS ARE GROWING CLAWS
YOUR HANDS ARE GROWING CLAWS

GIRLS SHOULD GO TO SLEEP
RACCOONS IN THE DEEP
WATCHING OVER YOU
I'LL BE WATCHING TOO
WE'LL ALL BE WATCHING YOU

(**JOEY** *stirs, furrowing her brow, tired, holding his hand.*)

JOEY. Dad?

TOM. Hey Jo.

JOEY. I was running.

TOM. I know.

JOEY. I ran really far.

TOM. Why'd you do that, Jo?

JOEY. I don't know.

TOM. I wish you wouldn't do that.

JOEY. I don't want to go.

TOM. What's that?

JOEY. I don't want to go to Berlin.

TOM. *(Surprised.)* That's... – You don't have to.

JOEY. Don't be mad.

TOM. *(Quiet.)* I'm not mad. Why would I be mad?

JOEY. Don't be mad.

(*He doesn't know what to say.*)

TOM. *(Shaking his head.)* Joey...

...Listen, hon... Your mom's gonna come, and when she gets here, we should all talk, okay?

JOEY. What do we have to talk about?

TOM. ...Well I'm just worried, 'cause you're starting up some of your old tricks, so...we just need to figure out what we're gonna do about it.

JOEY. Euughhh. I don't want to.

TOM. I know, I know.

> *(Rubbing his hands over his face, shaking his head, laughing sadly.)*

Ohhhhhh Joey you're killing me, darlin'.

JOEY. I know.

TOM. You're killing me.

> *(They hold hands.)*

***

15.

(**RAY** *and* **CARVER** *climb the porch with groceries.* **RAY** *stops at the threshold.*)

CARVER. You okay?

RAY. Yeah.

CARVER. You sure?

RAY. Yeah.

> (*She lowers herself down onto the porch and absently examines a big scrape running down the side of her leg, running her finger back and forth over the small beads of congealed blood.* **CARVER** *watches her for a second, then comes to sit next to her.*)

CARVER. ...That's a nasty scrape.

RAY. I know.

CARVER. What happened there?

RAY. Uhhhhh probably when Dad and I were running to get to the car – There's that thorn bush by the side of the house, / so...

CARVER. Right.

> (*She runs her finger over the scrape again, quiet. He watches her.*)

She's gonna be okay.

RAY. Yeahhh.

> (*Tracing her scrape, she shakes her head.*)

This one summer we decided we should be blood sisters, I think because we watched *Stand by Me* a million times in a row...and we actually stabbed each other in the hand with Dad's Swiss Army knife.

CARVER. Oh god.

RAY. Like for some reason we didn't realize we already shared the same blood. So she cut me, and I cried. And then I cut her, and she didn't even make a sound, she just – total, stoic, like – nothing. Nothing.

CARVER. Has she done something like this before?

RAY. Uhhhh. Yeah. She's had some pretty self-destructive spells, / so.

CARVER. Right.

RAY. It's just – endless.

CARVER. Yeah.

(She smiles sadly at him. He nods.)

RAY. ...You must be a good counselor.

CARVER. ...Oh – god, I don't know.

RAY. I'm sure you are.

CARVER. Well, thank you. Sometimes I think I like talking to people more than they like talking to me.

RAY. You know my dad's just really proud and can be / an asshole –

CARVER. No, I know – I just worry sometimes people are helping me more than I'm helping them, so –

RAY. / Oh, no –

CARVER. But I'm kind of a sad dude sometimes! So –. I get attached to folks when I shouldn't.

RAY. Right.

(A small pause.)

CARVER. I'm sure you know about Father Caldwell.

RAY. ...Yeah.

CARVER. ...So.

...I honestly just liked going over to his house. He'd make me food and ask me about school, and it was always so clean? – In his house. I don't know.

(She nods, looking at him.)

RAY. I remember you playing at the Senior Dance.

CARVER. Whaaaat?

RAY. With the Moonlight Miles. You and Nick Bauer and all them.

CARVER. Yeah. You were there?

RAY. They let the seventh-graders come for the first hour of it.

CARVER. *(Laughing.)* Oh, okay. Wow.

RAY. Yeah, I was the awkward girl squeezed into one of my mom's old dresses and trying to blend in with the wall, I can't believe you didn't notice me.

> *(He laughs.)*

So you don't play anymore?

CARVER. Uhhh – no.

> *(He nods, then looks at his hands. She watches him.)*

RAY. You played that one song – at the dance, I mean, I know you played a bunch of songs, but it was the one that you sang?

CARVER. Oh god, uhhh –

RAY. It was like – augh, I can't quite do it, but, like, um –

> *(She grabs Bobby's guitar, humming to herself and strumming, eyes closed.)*

HM HM
EVERYTHING'S GONNA BE ALRIGHT...

CARVER. *(Laughing.)* Auuughhhh, shit!

RAY. Do you – I mean it was something / like that –

CARVER. Yeah, no, I – remember.

RAY. That is a great. Song.

CARVER. *(Shaking his head.)* WHY do you remember that?

RAY. BECAUSE! Because. I was standing in the back being a seventh-grader and it was one of the first times I got swept up – You know when you're just starting to listen to your own music, and not your parents' music, and you're starting to – I don't know, you feel that swelling feeling – like, / you know –

CARVER. Yeah, I – know what / you mean.

RAY. Yeah! – So you were singing that song and that bursting feeling happened to me and... I don't know – I don't know how to describe it other than...something broke open in me. Which is the worst thing I've ever said, but – yeah.

CARVER. Wow.

RAY. Anyway / –

CARVER. I used to uhh… I'd break into my dad's records when Mom was working, before she got real bad off. She hid them under all this shit in her closet and I would dig them out – Blood on the Tracks, especially, I remember the first time I heard that line, um – "And I've never gotten used to it, I've just learned to turn it off" –

RAY. Oh yeah yeah / YEAH.

CARVER. Yeah. Yeah. That kinda made my world crack open.

RAY. Yeah.

But, so how does it go – that song?

CARVER. I don't know, Ray!

RAY. You remember it, though?

CARVER. I – yeah, I –

RAY. So how does it go?

CARVER. Aughhh shit, um…

RAY.

HM HM HM THEY DON'T THINK WE CAN MAKE IT…

CARVER. Uhhhhhh god, um…

> (**RAY** *offers him the guitar. He hesitates, then carefully takes it, finding his place.*)
>
> (*Timid, he talks through the first few lines of "Carver's Song."*)
>
> (*Then he sings, laughing a little through it.*)
>
> (*Then, at some point, he really lets go and plays, and there is a moment when the world drops away, changes, breaks open.*)

CARVER.

MY FATHER WAS BORN IN THIS TOWN
HE'S GONNA DIE HERE TOO

THERE'S A SEAT AT THE BAR
HE'S HOLDING IT FOR YOU
THEY ALL THINK WE'LL TAKE IT
THEY DON'T THINK WE CAN MAKE IT
THEY DON'T THINK WE CAN MAKE IT

I KNOW YOU BY THE PAIN THAT'S IN YOUR CHEST
I KNOW YOUR FATHER THINKS THAT HE KNOWS BEST
THEY WON'T SEE US COMING
OH, I LEFT THE CAR RUNNING
OH, I LEFT THE CAR RUNNING

BABY IT'S OUR NIGHT
BABY IT'S OUR NIGHT
EVERYTHING IS GONNA BE ALRIGHT
EVERYTHING IS GONNA BE ALRIGHT
HOLD ON TO ME TIGHT
WE CAN RUN AWAY
RUN AWAY

WE WERE BORN IN THIS TOWN
BUT IT'S TOO SMALL TO HOLD US LONG
WE'LL DRIVE ALL NIGHT
BEFORE THEY REALIZE WE'RE LONG GONE
'CAUSE WE DON'T HAVE TO TAKE IT
WE ARE THE ONES WHO CAN MAKE IT
WE ARE THE ONES WHO CAN MAKE IT

BABY IT'S OUR NIGHT
BABY IT'S OUR NIGHT
EVERYTHING IS GONNA BE ALRIGHT
EVERYTHING IS GONNA BE ALRIGHT
HOLD ON TO ME TIGHT
WE CAN RUN AWAY
RUN AWAY

CARVER & RAY.

WE'RE GONNA LIVE FOREVER
AND WHEN WE DIE WE'RE GONNA REMEMBER
THAT THIS NIGHT WAS FOR US
THAT THIS WAS OUR TIME

BABY IT'S OUR TIME

AH OOH
AH OOH
AH OOH
AH OOH

16.

(RAY, TOM, and JOEY sit on the porch. Nighttime. The crickets chirp. RAY plays and sings. TOM plays along, following the lyrics and chords written out on a small sheet of paper. JOEY sings along on the last verse, following a small sheet of paper held wrinkled in her hands.)

["Sea Anemones / Ray's Song"]

RAY.

I DRESSED UP LIKE A BIRD
BUT I WAS A WHALE
IN THE COURTYARD
AAH
TRYING SO HARD
TO LEARN THE GAME

SEA ANEMONES
MAKE THEIR ENEMIES
IN THE COURTYARD
TRYING SO HARD IN YOUR NAME

AND IT TAKES SOME TIME
IT TAKES SOME TIME
TO FIND YOU
IN THE LIVING ROOM

YOU ARE WAITING TILL DAWN
ALREADY GONE

TOM.

SEE THE LITTLE ONE
SEE HER WALKING HOME
IN THE MOONLIGHT
BY THE SUNLIGHT
SHE IS GROWN

RAY.

LOOK INTO HER FACE
LOOK INTO THE DARK
IT IS SHINING

    AAH
    ALL THE SHIMMER
    OF THE GREAT UNKNOWN

RAY & TOM.
    AND IT TOOK SOME TIME
    IT TOOK SOME TIME
    TO FIND HER
    UNDER CLAW AND FUR
    SHE WAS WAITING FOR ME
    SHE WAS FINDING HER KEY

RAY & JOEY.
    BIRDS LIVE ON THE SILL
    MEN WILL DRINK THEIR FILL
    WOMEN NEVER STAY
    THE MOON WILL HAVE HER SAY
    AND I WON'T RUN AWAY.

    (They sing. It's transcendent, somehow.)

    *(They talk quietly to each other as the song
    ends.)*

RAY. Good job, / Dad.

TOM. I know, not too / bad right?

JOEY. You did it, Dad.

TOM. I like that one, Miss Ray.

RAY. Yeah?

TOM. Yes.

    (The crickets chirp.)

End of Play